W9-CLA-196

3 1160 00332 598/

MOOSE
AND FRIENDS

For Charles Wilbur and Clifford Charles
and for the teachers and children
of Minnesota, South Dakota, and Wisconsin
—J.L.

To my mother, Cleo Partridge
—C.E.

Text copyright © 1993 by Jim Latimer
Illustrations copyright © 1993 by Carolyn Ewing

Charles Scribner's Sons Books for Young Readers
Macmillan Publishing Company • 866 Third Avenue, New York, NY 10022

Maxwell Macmillan Canada, Inc.
1200 Eglinton Avenue East, Suite 200, Don Mills, Ontario M3C 3N1

Macmillan Publishing Company is part of the
Maxwell Communication Group of Companies.

First Edition   10 9 8 7 6 5 4 3 2 1   Printed in Singapore

Library of Congress Cataloging-in-Publication Data
Latimer, Jim, date
Moose and friends / Jim Latimer;
pictures by Carolyn Ewing.   p.   cm.
Summary: Moose and his animal friends have four adventures in Moosewood.
ISBN 0-684-19335-3
[1. Moose—Fiction.   2. Animals—Fiction.]
I. Ewing, C. S., ill.   II. Title.
PZ7.L369617Mo   1992   [E]—dc20   91-14047

MOOSE AND FRIENDS

JIM LATIMER

Pictures by Carolyn Ewing

CHARLES SCRIBNER'S SONS • NEW YORK
Maxwell Macmillan Canada • Toronto
Maxwell Macmillan International
New York • Oxford • Singapore • Sydney

Fox's Pudding

Once, when Moose's beard was new and his antlers mostly velvet, he walked to the Post Office. Moose almost always passed by the Post Office because no one ever sent him a letter, because he did not know how to read, and because Armadillo, the postmaster, was not friendly. Armadillo was tired of mail, tired of valentines and Christmas cards, tired of animals in a hurry. Armadillo was tired of animals too hurried to say hello, and he told them so in a loud voice. He had told Moose so. But I am not in a hurry, Moose thought. I will stop and say hello to Armadillo.

Moose walked into the Post Office. Armadillo was sorting letters with his back to the door. Moose took a breath.

"Don't bother," Armadillo barked without looking up. "Don't bother to say hello," he said. "Your package is here, though. A package tied with string. It is a book," Armadillo said.

A book? A package? For Moose? Moose had never had a package or a book. He wondered how Armadillo knew it *was* a book, inside a package tied with string. He wondered how Armadillo knew it was he, Moose, without looking up or turning around. But he said simply, "I don't know how to read."

"It's a collection of recipes," Armadillo told him. "From Fox. Fox the peddler." Armadillo scowled. "Junk mail," he said. "And I don't have time to read it to you."

"Well, I would like to hear Moose's book," said Skunk. Skunk had come for her mail.

"We would like to hear it," said Newt and Frog. Newt and Frog had come for their mail, and Bear had come for his. Bear wanted to hear Moose's book, too.

Armadillo glared at them. "All right," he said. "I will read it."

Armadillo cleared his throat and began to read aloud from Fox's recipes. He read lists of woods and woody plants and lists of buds for browsing. Armadillo read about cottonwood and sourwood and buttonwood. And moosewood. He read about shrubs and sedges, herbs and grasses, and berries. Thimbleberries. Huckleberries. Gooseberries.

"And blueberries?" Moose asked him.

"And blueberries." Armadillo scowled. "And soup," he read. "Seed soup. Sedge soup. Sap soup. *And* bark, baked. And wood whipped-cream."

"Any cake?" asked Bear.

"And cake," Armadillo read. "Shrub shortcake. Pond pound cake. Leaf layer cake. And mousse."

"Moose?" Moose's eyes grew wide.

"Mousse," Armadillo told him. "Made with elm syrup. It's a French pudding."

Moose imagined a rich confection made with syrup and buttermilk— and blueberries.

"I would like to try a mousse," said Bear. Newt and Skunk said they would like to try it, and so did Frog. Armadillo admitted that *he* would like to try elm-syrup mousse, with whipped cream.

"But there *is* no elm-syrup mousse," Armadillo said. "There is no leaf layer cake, no sap soup, no baked bark," he said, "because Fox has made up all of these things." Armadillo bristled with indignation at the thought. "Fox makes things up," he told them, "because he is a peddler. Because he cannot help himself." Armadillo paused. "Fox would like you to buy the things in his book, the things in his recipes. But Fox doesn't know whether they will work. He has never baked bark or made mousse. All of these things," Armadillo concluded, "are junk."

Newt and Frog and Skunk and Bear and Moose stared at Armadillo. They could find no words to say. After a long moment, Moose turned away and walked out of the Post Office.

Moose found Fox standing beside his peddler's cart on the county road, his orange fur blazing. Fox greeted him with a wink and a wave. "GOOD MORNING," he shouted, hailing Moose with his paw. "It's wonderful to see you. Come and look."

In Fox's cart there were thimbleberries in jars. Also huckleberries and gooseberries. There was wood—sourwood and pepperwood. There were seeds and sedges for soup and shrubs for cake. Fox looked at Moose shrewdly.

"Today's special," he said, "is mousse mix with syrup—and everything you need for French pudding."

Moose asked Fox whether he had mailed him a book. Fox, beaming, admitted he had. "I am the author," Fox admitted.

"Armadillo says it is junk mail," Moose told him. "Armadillo says all of the things in the book are junk."

Fox's expression went blank. His eyes widened.

"Armadillo says elm-syrup mousse is not real," Moose said. "He says shrub shortcake and leaf layer cake and pond pound cake—all of your things—are made up. He says you do not know whether they will work."

Fox was crestfallen. "I tried them in my mind," he said, and fell silent. "Armadillo said my recipes are junk?" he asked after a long moment.

Moose nodded.

Fox looked at his paws. His ears dropped. Fox's fur seemed to wilt. He looked awful.

Now Moose felt awful. "But, Fox," he said, remembering how it had felt to receive a package tied with string, "*I* like your book. Skunk likes it, too."

Fox looked worse.

"*Bear* likes your recipes," Moose said, and he thought a moment. "Bear would like to make your mousse."

Fox lifted his eyes.

Moose and Fox found Newt and Frog, Skunk and Bear and Armadillo, in Armadillo's kitchen. Together they mixed a mousse from Fox's recipe, adding blueberries and root beer—and wood whipped-cream. When it was finished it *was* a pudding. It was a mousse.

"Good," said Skunk.

"It's good," Armadillo muttered with his mouth full.

"Good," agreed Newt and Frog, Moose and Bear.

Fox beamed. "It is real," he said.

Fox lifted his ears. His fur flared. Fox ate one whole quart of His Own Real Elm-Syrup Mousse—with Newt and Frog, Moose and Armadillo, and Skunk and Bear—going His Moose Way Home.

Whistle

On Valentine's Day, Skunk found Moose standing under a tree, his antlers in the branches, his mind—somewhere.

"MOOSE," she shouted, "I have a surprise—a valentine."

Moose blinked at her.

"I can whistle," Skunk told him. "I have been practicing."

Moose did not know how to whistle, though he had always wanted to. He wondered how Skunk had figured it out. "Let's hear," he said.

Skunk knit her brows. She formed a small opening with her mouth. She pushed the edge of her tongue against her bottom teeth, and then she blew.

Moose stared at her.

Skunk blew again. She blew a third time—many more times, but no whistle came.

"I forgot how," she told Moose. Skunk looked very disappointed.

Moose thought a moment. "Just wait," he said.

Moose galloped to the Animal Store and asked Newt, one of the storekeepers, whether she or Frog could whistle.

"Newts never whistle," Newt told him. "Frogs do make a throat sound," she said, "but it is not a whistle. Try Bear."

Moose tried Bear.

"Try Crow," Bear told him. "Bears woof. Or else they roar."

Crow told Moose crows only caw, and Armadillo would not say what armadillos do. "But," said Armadillo, "cardinals whistle. Just ask Cardinal."

Moose did not know Cardinal, but she was whistling when he found her. Moose told her that Skunk had learned to whistle and then forgot.

"You try," said Cardinal.

Moose tried. He puckered—and honked.

"Flute your tongue," Cardinal told him.

Moose fluted his tongue. He puckered his muzzle and blew—and sort of hummed. And then he whistled. It was almost easy.

"Good," said Cardinal.

Moose thanked Cardinal and galloped back to the place where he had left his friend. He found her sitting beside a bush, looking gloomy.

"Flute your tongue," he said.

Skunk stared at him. She fluted her tongue, puckered, and blew—and sort of hummed, and then whistled. Skunk's whistle splashed out onto the wind. It skipped over stones and echoed around rocks and trees. Skunk whistled for one half hour without stopping.

"Good," said Moose.

"You try," said Skunk.

Moose whistled a deep, bell-sounding, cardinal's whistle.

Skunk, her eyes wide, listened in silence. She had never dreamed or imagined a whistle like this. It was beautiful. *Moose* was beautiful.

"Moose," she said, "will you marry me? I mean—will you be my valentine?"

Moose nodded, whistling. He told Skunk he liked her whistle. "It echoes," he said.

Skunk and Moose whistled together without stopping all the rest of Valentine's Day, going Their Moose Way Home.

Halloween

On Halloween, Moose saw an animal, fierce and black, with a broom and a witch's hat. Moose squinted, steadying his long legs and focusing his eyes. It is a witch, he thought. And then he saw a pale creature, ghost-white, with mean eyes. The creature woofed like a ghost, then roared. Moose shivered. "It is a ghost," he said. His mother had warned him about them. And there were two more animals, very fierce, with dwarf beards and dwarf shoes, dwarf hoods and dwarf belt buckles. They were carrying axes, the kind dwarves carry. Moose was tall, not quite seven feet and almost seven hundred pounds, but he was afraid of witches, dwarves, and ghosts. He turned to run, but the witch, the dwarves, and the ghost were coming closer. Moose was surrounded. He could not run away.

"Help," Moose whispered, then shouted: "HELP!" And then the witch took off her hat. It was Skunk, his friend, dressed for Halloween. Then the ghost brushed off his fur. It was Bear with his fur floured white, woofing and roaring and making his eyes mean for Halloween. And then the dwarves lifted off their beards. They were the storekeepers, Newt and Frog, dressed in belts and beards for Halloween.

I would like to dress for Halloween, Moose thought. He stretched his tail and gave it a witch-broom swish. But Moose's tail did not look like a witch's broom. It looked like a tail. Moose bristled his fur to look like a ghost. He woofed and made his eyes look mean. But Moose's woof did not sound like a ghost's. His bristled fur made him look like a hairbrush—like a moose who has *seen* a ghost.

Moose did not look like a witch. He did not look or sound like a ghost. He shook his head, doubting he could be a dwarf, and shook his head again, swishing his beard. Swishing his beard from side to side. From side to side. Moose's beard. Moose suddenly raised his head, lifting his long ears. He *had* a beard, built in. A beard as good as any dwarf's. Moose thought, I will be a dwarf for Halloween, but then his heart fell. He did not have a hood. He did not have a belt. He did not have an ax or shoes.

Skunk, Moose's friend, was a collector. She collected . . . Moose wasn't sure what. Scarves, he thought, and bracelets, and parts of clocks, and broken bells. Maybe Skunk would have a *hood*. Moose brightened. Maybe she would have a dwarf's ax. He went to see.

Skunk did not have a dwarf's hood or an ax. She did not have a dwarf's belt or shoes. She had bells and bracelets and parts of clocks. And she had—a parachute.

Moose *was* a dwarf for Halloween, not quite seven feet tall and almost seven hundred pounds—a *tall* dwarf on sturdy hooves and loose long legs, a dwarf with a beard *and* a hood (Skunk's parachute), going His Moose Way Home.

A Calm Song on the Trombone

November again. Moose's birthday again. Moose sniffed the November, birthday air. He shuffled through the bright, November snow. Soon it would be Thanksgiving, then Hanukkah. Then it would be winter. And then Christmas. Moose blinked. It felt like winter already.

For his birthday, Skunk sewed Moose a dark tie with flowers, red lilies or red azaleas, with lovely blue-green leaves and stems. Skunk sewed Moose's tie on her machine, a little crooked, but it was lovely. Moose put it on. Skunk tied it for him. Moose did not take Skunk's tie off.

"You like it," Skunk said afterward. "You wear it every day."

"Yes," said Moose. He wore Skunk's tie every day because he liked it, and because it is hard to untie a tie with hooves.

It was hard to pick blueberries with hooves, hard to walk on walls, and open bottles, but with hooves you could play the trombone. On his birthday, though Moose had never seen a trombone and did not have a trombone, Crow gave him a gold trombone mouthpiece.

"You can play trombone with moose hooves," Crow told him, "and with a good strong muzzle, called an embouchure, which you have," said Crow. "Trombone is a perfect instrument for you."

Moose liked band music. He liked the crackle and blare of the brass. He liked his trombone mouthpiece and his flower tie. And on the Saturday after his birthday, Skunk and Crow found Moose a whole trombone, dinged a little and a little bent, but gold-colored, matching his mouthpiece. It was perfect for a moose. Before Thanksgiving, before Hanukkah or Christmas, long, loud trombone notes echoed through Moosewood. The forest rang with a sound like ships at sea, with a sound like steam engines. Moose was wearing Skunk's tie, playing trombone, when Cricket, Muskrat, and Opossum found him on New Year's Eve.

"You're awake?" Moose asked when he saw them, putting his trombone aside. Muskrat nodded. She and Cricket and Opossum slept during the winter, but they sometimes woke up to build figures out of snow. "Snowmen" they called them, though they were usually figures of animals.

"Someone knocked our snowman down," Muskrat told Moose.

Moose looked at her.

"A tall creature," said Cricket. "With big footprints," she said. "Big hoof footprints."

"A creature taller than you," said Muskrat.

"With big hooves and a purse," said Cricket.

"A *purse*?" Moose asked, his eyes wide.

"A purse as big as a suitcase," Cricket told him.

"Actually it *is* a suitcase," said Muskrat, "filled with lost balls and kite string. Because in summer, the tall creature cuts kite string, so your kite flies away and is lost forever, but she saves the string. And do you know how sometimes in the summer you're playing ball and you think your ball is lost?"

Moose nodded.

"Well, it isn't lost," Muskrat said. "The tall creature hides it. Then she steals it."

"And she drinks a lot of soda pop," said Cricket.

"Quarts and gallons," said Muskrat. "Her favorite flavors are sour and virus."

"And prune," added Cricket. "And witch Kool-Aid."

"The tall creature likes things that are awful," Opossum explained to Moose.

"She likes animals tripping when they're playing tag," Cricket explained. Cricket thought a moment. "Probably she trips them herself," she said.

"And she likes," said Muskrat, "high temperatures and toothaches. She likes the lines busy when you're trying to make a call. Actually," Muskrat decided, "*she* calls, from a phone booth, to *make* the lines busy."

"She has Troll for a friend," Cricket said. "And she likes canceled birthdays and dark Saturdays and torn valentines and nothing for Hanukkah and nothing for Christmas and—and puppies."

Puppies. Moose and Muskrat stared at Cricket. "But puppies aren't awful," Muskrat said.

Cricket looked confused.

"Maybe," said Opossum, "puppies could be her weakness."

There was a moment of quiet while Cricket and Moose and Muskrat thought about this.

"And in winter," Moose said, "she knocks down snowmen."

Opossum, Cricket, and Muskrat nodded.

Moose couldn't imagine a tall creature with a suitcase, who liked prune pop and puppies, who knocked down snowmen. He had better go and see, he decided. He had better go and look at the big footprints. Moose took apart his trombone and zippered it away. He lowered his head. Cricket, Muskrat, and Opossum scrambled onto his back. Together they set out for Cricket's Clearing.

Moose plunged through the bright snow, leaving a crumpled trail.

In Cricket's Clearing a fine snow-figure—it must once have been a fine figure, Moose thought—lay toppled and scattered about. There were footprints, hoofprints, on the clearing floor, and here and there were marks, unmistakable, of a big suitcase. For a long time Cricket, Muskrat, Moose, and Opossum stood staring at the wrecked figure and footprints and suitcase marks.

"I wonder . . ." Moose said, still staring.

"No," said Muskrat, apparently reading Moose's thoughts. "There is no way this tall creature will ever change. There is no way she will say she is sorry or promise to be good."

"No way," Cricket agreed. "She was born mean. A creature with big hooves and a suitcase who likes virus soda pop will always be mean."

"Except for the puppies," said Opossum.

There was another long silence.

"Maybe," said Moose, "if we played music for her, she would change." Opossum thought about it. "But it would have to be music played very softly on the violin," she said. "And it would have to be a calm song."

"It would have to be for free," added Cricket. "You would have to play for her for free."

"And it *couldn't* be trombone," added Muskrat, reading Moose's thoughts again.

Moose promised Muskrat, Cricket, and Opossum he would watch for a tall creature with a suitcase. He turned to go, wishing them a happy New Year, then turned back. "Apart from her suitcase and hooves," Moose asked, "what does the creature look like, do you think?"

"Possibly a goat," said Cricket.

"Or possibly a sheep," said Muskrat. "I think a long-haired sheep."

Much later, at sunset—almost sunset—Moose stood with his trombone in the shadow of a tall tree. He was wearing his tie. He stood listening, his trombone in its zippered case beside him. Someone, or something, was lurking near him in the shadows. The thing was tall, with long fur and sheep horns. It stood on hooves, upright. The thing waited. Moose waited. The sun went down. The moon came out. And then the thing crept out of the shadows.

It rose up and stood, tall and erect in the moon-glittered snow. Its secret eyes flashed in the moonlight as it searched from side to side. The creature *was* tall—tall and graceful, with a silky coat and curving horns. A Barbary sheep, Moose thought. A tall Barbary sheep with a big suitcase. The Barbary sheep set out through the snow, lifting her hooves high, carrying her suitcase above her head. She was heading toward the county road, in the direction of Cricket's Clearing. Moose followed her quietly, staying near the shadows, bringing his trombone.

The silk-furred animal stalked along the county road, openly now, a tall, sheep figure in the moonlight. Moose stayed close to the shadows, following, until, together, Moose and the Barbary sheep came to Cricket's Clearing.

Cricket, Muskrat, and Opossum were nowhere to be seen, but they had built their figure—their snowman—again. Moose stopped to stare, almost overcome with admiration. Cricket, Muskrat, and Opossum were good. The figure was wonderfully real. It was a warrior, a viking or a fierce sea captain. The figure stood, brave and tall in the moonlight. The tall Barbary sheep was staring, too.

Moose walked closer—not too close. He sat down quietly. He unzipped his case, took out the pieces of his trombone, and put them together. Moose sat, erect and very tall, supporting his instrument on his shoulder. The Barbary sheep stood beside the snow figure. She lifted her suitcase above her head, as if to strike the snowman. And then she hesitated, apparently sensing something or someone near. And then Moose played a note, a long, lovely note on the trombone.

Moose's note sounded like a strong steam whistle, like a ship's whistle or a train whistle, but he played softly. Moose played a calm song very softly for the Barbary sheep, and he played for her for free. The sheep lowered her suitcase. The tall creature turned and stared and there was Moose, playing the slide trombone in the moonlight and wearing Skunk's flower tie. Though Moose's music was very calm and soft, the sheep did not look calm. There was panic in her eyes. She put down her suitcase. Moose stopped playing his trombone. He opened his mouth to ask the sheep about puppies and prune pop, but she seemed to bleat at him. The Barbary sheep stuttered and took a step back.

"I—I promise to be good," she said. The tall sheep promised to change, promised never to knock down snowmen, and then, lifting her silky hooves, she goat-galloped away along the county road. Moose watched until the sheep was lost from sight. She had left her big suitcase behind.

On the second day of February, Cricket, Muskrat, and Opossum woke up to look for shadows. Moose told them the story of the tall sheep in the February sunshine. He had brought the sheep's big suitcase with him. Together, Cricket, Muskrat, Opossum, and Moose opened the suitcase. There were lost balls inside. Also kite strings and prune pop. And pictures of puppies—mostly cocker spaniels but some Airedales and collies.

"You played your trombone?" Cricket asked when they had looked at the suitcase for a while.

Moose nodded. "I played a calm song," he said.

"A lullaby?" asked Opossum.

Moose nodded. "'Good Night, You Lovely Sheep,'" he said, "and 'Dear Sheep, I Am Dreaming of You,' and 'Lamb's Lullaby.'"

"*Three* songs," said Cricket.

"Well, it won't work," said Muskrat. "She will not stop stealing balls—hiding balls, then stealing them. She will not stop drinking soda, sour or virus. She will not stop knocking down snowmen. A calm song on the trombone will not change her," Muskrat said.

"No," said Cricket. "*Three* calm songs on the trombone—three lullabies—will not cause her to change."

"But," said Opossum, giving Moose a look, "three songs *might*."

On his way home Moose thought that calm music on the trombone, played very softly, played for free, might cause a Barbary sheep to change. But would it, though? Moose thought again. Maybe not, he decided, going His Moose Way Home.

But it *might*.